SEDUCTIVE CEO

by: Anasha Calani

Contents

Dedicated to my baby brother Andrew

Prologue

The Time - Modern Day

The Place - Arielle

Arielle was a picturesque town located right beside the sea. Several yachts and boats were bobbing up and down on the water. One of the yachts belonged to Dominic and Angie Cardenas. It was on this yacht that Dominic had proposed to Angie. In the summer, they would go sailing. In Arielle, people cared about each other. In the winter, during the holidays, it was beautifully decorated.

Chapter One

Kaue Rafael Araujo sat at his desk. It was the start of what he expected would be another long day. As the CEO of his company, Araujo Enterprises, he was used to working long hours. He stood up and went over to the coffee machine. As he sipped his coffee, he looked up at the sky. It was a dark steel gray. He reviewed his schedule at his desk; he had meetings all day. He took small comfort in the fact that it was Friday. He was already looking forward to the weekend. He had plans to clean his apartment. Kaue Araujo was a really good guy. He loved to support his parents and his two younger sisters. He was a man of truth and honor. He took pride in himself and in his work.

Chapter Two

Across town, Patricio Kayano and Cristiano Arias sat in a meeting in Patricio's top-floor office. It was just after eleven that Friday morning. The topic of their discussion was the upcoming gala. Cristiano leaned back in his chair and said to Patricio, "I can't believe the gala is only two weeks away." Patricio nodded and said, "Neither can I."

Patricio Kayano was a bit of a mama's boy. He loved his parents and his two younger sisters, Paloma and Patricia. Cristiano Arias was kind of a bad boy who turned into a good guy. He was very hardworking and driven.

Chapter Three

It was just after eight when Kaue decided to call it a day. After the long hours, he was quite tired. He just wanted to go home and relax with a nice hot meal. As soon as he stepped outside, he could feel a chill in the air. The temperature had dropped significantly since the last time he was outside. The night was turning misty, and the full moon drifted in and out of the clouds. As soon as he got home, he went straight to his bedroom and put on his dark blue sweatsuit. Returning to the kitchen, he sat at the counter and had dinner. Afterward, he went into his home office to check his emails. A short while later, he went to bed. It wasn't long before he fell asleep.

Chapter Four

Bright and early on Saturday morning, Adriana Conceicao was bustling around her boutique. As she expected it would be a busy day, she had scheduled extra help. It had always been her dream to have her own boutique. After the passing of her beloved grandfather, she had inherited a generous sum of money. She had used some of that money to open her boutique. Now, after six months, it was doing quite well. One of the factors that contributed to her success was the location. She was nestled right between the barber shop and the beauty salon.

Chapter Five

Saturday night was a boys' night out for Andre Bahiense, Bietio Cardoso, and Caio Domingos. The three men were best friends and had been since their first year of college. They had seen each other through a lot over the years: loss of a job, serious illness, or a painful breakup. On this particular night, the three men were celebrating the weekend. It had been a long week for all three, and now it was time to hang out and have a good time. After several hours of talking and laughing, the three men finally decided to call it a day. As soon as they stepped outside, it started to pour. After a few minutes, the rain slowed down enough for the men to run to their cars. One by one, they drove off.

Chapter Six

Two weeks later, it was once again time for the annual gala. All of Arielle was buzzing. The two happening spots on the morning of the gala were the beauty salon, which was owned by Janaina Conceicao, and Adriana's boutique. Adriana was quite pleased at how busy the boutique was. Since she opened the doors at nine, there had been nonstop traffic. It was only after three in the afternoon when it finally slowed down. At this time, Adriana went into the back room to get some more items.

Chapter Seven

This year, the gala was held at the Arielle Grand Hotel. The guests started arriving promptly at seven. Leonardo and Fernanda Kayano, their son Patricio, and his latest girlfriend were the first to arrive. Not long after, Santiago and Bibiana Araujo arrived. A good while later, Kauê Araujo walked in, looking extremely handsome in his dark blue tuxedo. His jet-black hair was combed back. A few minutes later, the Fab Four walked in. The Fab Four consisted of Alandra Ferreira, Alessandra Costa, Ana Freitas, and Anita Machado. All four were dressed alike in pale pink dresses. The Sensational Six came bubbling in. The six were Gracie and Janna Harlow, Neusa and Niceta Araujo, and Paloma and Patricia Kayano.

Chapter Eight

By eight, the party was in full swing, and everybody was in a great mood. By this time, dinner and then dessert had been served. The band was playing some lively tunes. The gala was a great opportunity for people to catch up with each other. People were moving around and mingling. A few minutes after nine, he came in. Several young ladies turned to look at him as soon as he walked in. He was deeply tanned and gorgeous. His dark brown hair was combed back, and he wore a dark purple tuxedo and matching shoes. His name was Cisco Daza Cardenas. Gracie took one look at him and said excitedly to her little sister, Janna, who was seated beside her, "Look at that handsome guy." Janna looked where Gracie was pointing and said to Gracie, "Who is that?" Just then, the Fab Four came over to their table. Now, the fact of the matter is that there had always been somewhat of a rivalry between the Sensational Six and the Fab Four.

Chapter Nine

Just after midnight, the guests started slowly making their way out. Several had made reservations to stay overnight, so they went up to their rooms. The Fab Four were all worn out from the party, so they went up to their suite. They spent the next several hours eating snacks and talking about cute boys. It was just after two in the morning when they all fell asleep.

Chapter Ten

A few days later, Cisco called Janna. When she answered, he said, "Hey, this is Cisco Cardenas. I was hoping I'd get you."

Janna smiled to herself. Ever since the gala, she had been thinking about him and secretly hoping he would call. She sat at the kitchen counter and said, "Hey, Cisco."

He replied in his sexy, velvet voice, "Hi, sweetie. What are you up to?"

Janna glanced around her and said, "Oh, not much. How about you?"

Cisco said, "Well, I have to fly up to Bellanville for my parents' anniversary on Saturday."

Janna responded, "Oh, that sounds like fun."

Cisco tried to sound enthusiastic as he said, "Yeah, big fun."

After a brief silence, Cisco asked Janna, "Hey, why don't you come with me?"

Janna was glad she was sitting down. She asked him, "Isn't it going to be a family affair?"

Cisco replied, "Yes, but I'd like you to come with me."

Janna thought for a long minute, then said, "Okay, I'll come."

Cisco said, "Great. I'll call you back with the details."

Janna replied, "Okay."

Just then, Janna received a call from her sister. She said to Cisco, "Call me later."

Cisco said, "Absolutely."

Both hung up.

Chapter Eleven

Cisco Cardenas was a very powerful young man. He was also very driven. After graduating with his bachelor's in Economics from a top college, he continued on to receive his MBA. Now, he was the CEO of his company, Cardenas Enterprises. To a lot of very important people, he was a young man on the rise.

Despite all of his professional success, the one area he hadn't been lucky in so far was love. A few times, he had come close, but just when he was starting to care for a young lady, things wouldn't work out. He hoped for the day when he would find Mrs. Right.

It was just after seven on Saturday morning when Cisco called Janna. He said, "Hey, sweetie, I'll pick you up in fifteen minutes." Janna replied, "Okay, I'll be ready."

Chapter Twelve

As soon as they pulled up in front of the plane, Janna said to Cisco, "Wow, is that yours?"

Cisco grinned and said, "Yes, it is."

As they were walking to the plane, Cisco's long-time pilot, Ralph, said to him, "Welcome, Mr. Cardenas."

Cisco said, "Good morning, Ralph."

Cisco and Janna boarded the plane. Janna looked around and said, "This is so nice."

Cisco nodded and said, "Yeah, it is."

The plane was quite spacious, with plenty of room to move around. During the flight, Cisco sat beside Janna. An hour later, the plane landed at Belleville Airport. It was just after twelve.

Cisco and Janna got off and walked to their waiting limo. During the drive, Cisco pulled Janna into his arms for a very passionate kiss. Janna wrapped her arms around his neck as she returned his kisses. Cisco made no hesitation in letting her know his intentions.

Forty minutes later, they pulled up in front of the Cardenas mansion. Janna looked and said to Cisco, "Wow."

Cisco said, "Yeah, I know."

As soon as they got out of the limo, the front door opened, and his mother, Angie, came running out. She ran to him, threw her arms around him, and said, "Oh, my baby boy is home."

He embraced her and said, "Hi, Mom."

He turned to Janna and said, "Janna, this is my mother. Mom, this is Janna."

Angie hugged Janna and said, "Hi, dear, welcome."

Janna hugged her and said, "Thank you."

Just then, his father, Dominic, came out. He hugged Cisco and said, "Welcome home, son."

Cisco said, "Hi, Dad." He said to Janna, "Janna, this is my dad. Dad, this is Janna."

They went inside to the living room. Through the sliding glass doors, they could see the Olympic-size pool. After a light snack...

Chapter Thirteen

For the next several months, Cisco and Janna's relationship was in high gear. Janna was enjoying all of Cisco's attention. For his part, Cisco was having a good time with Janna. She was quite unlike the other women he had dated. However, despite all their happiness, a ghost from Cisco's past was about to make her arrival.

Chapter Fourteen

Meanwhile, back in Arielle, it was business as usual for Kaue Araujo. Bright and early on Monday, he was at his desk. A few minutes after eleven, he held a meeting with his staff in the conference room. He stood in the front and watched as his staff slowly made their way in. Very soon, there was standing room only.

Once everyone was in, he called the meeting to order. As he was speaking, he maintained eye contact with his staff. Some were very attentive, while others seemed distracted.

Afterward, some of his staff commended him on his speech. Kaue had always prided himself on being an effective leader.

Chapter Fifteen

Patricio Kayano and his assistant, Cristiano Arias, sat in a meeting. It was the norm for the two men to discuss the plans for the week.

Cristiano had now been working for Patricio for the past six months. Right away, Patricio could tell that Cristiano was extremely hardworking and driven. Cristiano rose to the occasion with every task and did his job extremely well.

It had been a great day when Cristiano walked into Patricio's office. Patricio had been looking for an assistant. After one interview, Patricio offered Cristiano the job. Now, Cristiano was invaluable.

Chapter Sixteen

Enter Arlette Vieira. Several years earlier, Arlette and Cisco had been in a serious relationship. Several times, Arlette had expected that Cisco would propose. As it turned out, that did not happen. Instead, Cisco abruptly ended their relationship.

As Arlette sat in her living room, she thought back to that last night. They had gone out to eat at a very romantic restaurant. Afterward, they had gone back to Cisco's penthouse. Just when she thought he was going to propose, he had said to her, "I think it's time we break up."

Arlette had been completely blindsided. She stood up and said to him, "You really are a bastard." With that, she left. As she sat in her car, she calmed down and drove home. Now, she was determined to get him back.

Chapter Seventeen

Just when Cisco thought things were going well, a ghost from his past came. As he was out jogging early the morning after the party, he happened to run into Arlette. She said to him, "Well, well. If it isn't Cisco Cardenas."

At first, Cisco couldn't place her. He said, "I'm sorry. Do I know you?"

She stomped her foot and said, "Don't you dare play dumb with me. It's Arlette."

Cisco looked around and then said to Arlette, "Maybe there is a better place we can talk."

Chapter Eighteen

Here's the corrected passage:

During the flight home, Janna noticed that Cisco seemed distracted. She said to him quietly, "Is everything okay?"

Cisco had been staring out the window. He looked at her and said, "Yeah. Why?"

Janna glanced around and then said to him, "You seem far away."

Cisco said, "Oh, I just have a lot on my mind."

Janna knew better than to push. She said to Cisco, "If you want to talk, I'm here."

Cisco reached over, took her hand in his, and kissed it. He said to her, "You comfort me."

Janna smiled and said, "That's what I'm here for."

Chapter Nineteen

Two days later, Cisco was sitting at his desk thinking about the night before last. He and Janna had had the most romantic dinner. He was starting to think that Janna could be the one for him.

A knock on the door quickly brought him back to the present. When he looked up, he was surprised and somewhat annoyed to see Arlette. He asked her, "Now, what the hell do you want?"

As Arlette walked toward him, she said, "Well, it's nice to see you too, Cisco."

Cisco loosened his tie and then said, "What the hell do you want?"

She came and sat on the edge of his desk and said, "I want answers for why you broke my heart all those years ago."

Cisco said, "That was a long time ago. You should be over it by now."

This was not at all what Arlette wanted to hear. She said to Cisco, "You really are an insensitive bastard."

Cisco said, "Why don't you just get the hell out of my office?"

With that, she stormed out.

Chapter Twenty

Arlette sat at the kitchen counter, still quite upset by Cisco's words to her. She had been hoping for an explanation or at least an apology. As it turned out, Cisco had given her neither.

She slowly started to think that Cisco might have been right. It had been a while since they had broken up; maybe it was time for her to move on. With this new thought, she began to feel better. She decided then and there that she was no longer going to dwell on Cisco Cardenas.

Chapter Twenty-One

Two days later, Defelice Saachi called Cisco. Defelice and Cisco had met on their first day of college. Right away, they became good friends.

Defelice said to him, "Well, it's about time I reached you."

Cisco said, "Yeah, I've been busy. I'm dealing with some stuff right now."

Right away, Defelice could tell that something was bothering Cisco. It had been the same all those many years ago when they were in college.

Defelice said to him, "Hey, listen, I'll be in town on Friday. We can do dinner."

Cisco said, "That sounds good."

Chapter Twenty-Two

It had now been two weeks since Janna had spoken to or seen Cisco. The last time they were together, he had seemed very distant. She suddenly wondered if there was someone else in his life. It had happened to her several times before she met a guy she liked, but just when things were going well, the guy would dump her for another girl.

She made up her mind then and there that she was not about to let some guy run her life, not even Cisco Cardenas. She suddenly felt empowered.

Chapter Twenty-Three

It was a guys' night out for Horacio Conceicao, Emanuel Correia, Jose Ferreira, and Julio Costa. It was the norm for the four men to hang out. Their spot was the trendy new nightclub owned by Leonardo and Lia Machado. Leonardo and Lia were attorneys turned entrepreneurs. Two months ago, they opened Machado's, and now it is doing quite well.

As the four men walked in, Lia called to them, "Hey, boys."

Horacio smiled at her as they walked to a booth in the far corner. Over snacks and seltzer water, the four men had a good time catching up with each other. Just after ten, Jose glanced at his watch and said, "Wow, I didn't realize it was that late. I should get going."

Julio, who had been sitting beside him, said, "I should go too." The four men said their goodbyes and headed out.

As they stepped outside, it started to rain—lightly at first, but then it began to pour. All four men ran to their car and left.

Chapter Twenty-Four

Cisco Cardenas and Defelice Saachi sat at a quiet table. A few other people were seated at nearby tables, and everyone was deep in conversation.

Over dinner, Defelice asked Cisco, "So what's up?"

Cisco knew there was no sense in keeping anything from Defelice. It had been the same when they were in college. Cisco said to Defelice, "I've been seeing this young lady, and I really like her. I can tell she really likes me, too."

Defelice nodded and then asked him, "So what's the problem?"

Cisco said, "My ex is trying to make trouble."

Defelice sat up straight in his chair and said, "Listen to me. I say you should tell your ex that you're very happy with your new girlfriend and you just want her to leave you two alone."

Cisco leaned back in his chair and said, "I'm worried that the girl I like won't want to see me again."

Defelice said, "Don't think like that. If she really likes you, then she'll give you and your relationship another chance."

Just then, Defelice's cell phone rang. He said to Cisco, "I have to take this." He got up and walked outside.

Cisco glanced at his watch and then motioned to the server for the check. A few minutes later, Defelice came back in and said to Cisco, "Listen, I'm sorry, but I have to go."

Cisco stood up and said, "Oh, don't worry. I'm about to head out now, too."

Defelice said to him, "Just remember what I've said."

Cisco said, "I will. Thank you." Then, both men left.

Chapter Twenty-Five

There was a storm brewing. Lives were about to be shaken up. It started on a warm day in Arielle. At six that morning, Dominic Cardenas was out jogging. He just happened to bump into a certain young lady.

He said, "Oh, I'm sorry. Please excuse me."

She smiled and said, "Oh, don't worry about it."

He said to her, "I don't believe we've met. I'm Dominic Cardenas. And you are?"

She replied, "I'm Chiara Saachi."

He lowered his mouth to kiss her hand. Unbeknownst to the two of them, they were being observed by Jacey Arias, who just happened to be out jogging at that time. Jacey stood at a distance, and afterward, she went on her way.

As a good friend of Angie Cardenas, she felt she should tell Angie what she saw. As she entered her home, Elonzo greeted her with a kiss and said, "Hey, baby."

Jacey said, "Hi, honey."

Elonzo took one look at her and could tell that something was bothering her. He asked her, "What's wrong?"

Jacey said, "Well, I was just out jogging, and I observed Dominic Cardenas kissing some young lady's hand."

Elonzo asked her, "Who's the young lady?"

Jacey sat on a stool at the kitchen counter and said, "I have no idea, but I'm tempted to tell Angie."

Elonzo said, "Don't. You don't know the whole story. It could just be innocent."

Chapter Twenty-Six

A few days later, Cisco sat in his living room. He thought about what Defelice had said and decided he was right. He took out his phone and called Janna. When she answered, his heart skipped a beat.

He said to her, "Hey, baby."

Janna smiled to herself as she sat at the kitchen counter. She replied, "Hey, Cisco." The fact was, she had been secretly hoping he would call.

He said in his sexy, velvet voice, "I've been thinking about you and missing you."

Janna said, "I've been thinking about you too. I miss you as well."

Chapter Twenty-Seven

 A few days later, Angie was sitting in the living room when her cell phone rang. It was her older brother.

She said, "Hey, big brother."

He replied, "Hey, Ang. Listen, I have some bad news. Grandma is quite ill. You'd best come."

Angie jumped up and said, "Yeah, okay. I can be there tomorrow."

Her brother said, "Alright."

As Angie hung up, her mind was racing. Right away, there were several things she needed to do. She went into the master bedroom she shared with Elonzo and headed straight to the walk-in closet. Tucked in the far corner was her burgundy luggage set. She took it out.

As she was packing, Elonzo came in and asked, "Hey, babe, what's going on?"

Angie said, "Mark called and said that Grandma is very ill and that I need to come."

Elonzo said, "Oh, I'm so sorry."

Angie replied, "I'm planning to leave early."

Chapter Twenty-Eight

It was at this time that lives were about to be shaken up. It was just after eight on Saturday night. Dominic Cardenas was out on his terrace. It was a warm night, and there was a full moon. Dominic stared out into the distance, thinking about Chiara Saachi. Ever since their encounter the other day, he had been thinking about her constantly.

Then his cell phone rang. It was Angie. He tried to sound excited as he said, "Hey, baby."

She said, "Hi, honey. How is everything?"

Dominic replied, "Things are going well here. How is your grandmother?"

Angie said, "Not so good. She has a fever, so we're watching her closely. I am thinking of staying longer."

Elonzo said, "Sure, babe. Just stay as long as you need to."

Angie said, "I will keep you posted."

Dominic said, "Please do."

After he hung up, he showered quickly and headed out. It was a fine night to hit the bar scene. He went straight to the trendy new nightclub. As soon as he walked in, he saw Chiara. He found a quiet booth and sat down.

A few minutes later, she very discreetly made her way over to him. As she sat down, he said softly, "Hey, baby girl."

She replied, "Hi, honey."

Dominic glanced around and then asked her, "Do you want to stay here or go back to my place?"

Chiara pretended to think momentarily and then said, "I think I want to go to your place."

They got up and made their way out. As soon as they got into Dominic's apartment, Chiara looked around and said, "This is so nice."

Dominic said, "Yes, it is." As he walked into the kitchen, he asked Chiara, "Can I get you a nightcap?"

Chiara sat on the white couch in the living room and said, "Yes, thank you."

Dominic came over and sat next to her on the couch. She found his strong cologne intoxicating while her perfume turned Dominic on. Just then, there was a loud clap of thunder, and the lights dimmed.

Chiara stood up and said, "I should go."

Dominic said to her, "It's too rainy. Just stay here tonight."

Chiara asked him, "Are you sure?"

Dominic took one step closer to her and said, "Yes, I am."

A short while later, Chiara was comfortably settled in the huge king-size bed in Dominic's bedroom. It wasn't long before she fell asleep. Meanwhile, Dominic was settled on the couch in the living room. As he lay there, he thought about Chiara.

Chapter Twenty-Nine

Chiara was up at eight the next morning. She made her way to the kitchen. As she stood at the stove making breakfast, Dominic came up behind her, wrapped his arms around her, and kissed the back of her neck. She turned in his arms. He leaned down and kissed her, lightly at first. Then their kisses deepened. He lifted her blouse over her head as she unzipped his jeans.

With their clothes in a heap on the floor, Dominic took her by the hand, led her into the bedroom, closed the door, and locked it. Very soon, things got even hotter as he laid her on the bed and claimed her.

Two hours later, they were both spent and quite satisfied. He pulled her into his arms and held her close. A short while later, there was a noise at the front door. Dominic jumped up and said to Chiara, "Someone is here. Hide in the closet." Chiara quickly got up and hid in the closet. Dominic ran into the kitchen, gathered up the clothes, and hid them in his home office. He opened the front door to see his son, Cisco.

Cisco said, "Good morning."

Dominic replied, "Morning."

Cisco looked around and asked him, "So what have you been up to?"

Dominic said, "Oh, nothing, just hanging around."

As they walked into the kitchen, Cisco asked, "Any update from Mom about Grandma?"

Dominic suddenly remembered Chiara in the bedroom closet. He said, "No, not today."

Dominic asked Cisco, "Have you eaten?"

Cisco sat at the kitchen counter and said, "Not yet, but I'm good."

After having a cup of coffee, Cisco stood up and said, "I'll be going now."

Dominic said, "Alright."

As they walked toward the front door, Dominic said to Cisco, "I'll keep you posted about Grandma."

Cisco replied, "Please do."

After Cisco left, Dominic locked the door and put the chain on. He ran into the bedroom and called to Chiara. She said, "I thought he would never leave."

Dominic said, "Yeah, I know."

Suddenly, both were in the mood again. Dominic closed the bedroom door and locked it. He laid Chiara on the bed, and they were intimate—once, twice, three times. Afterward, Chiara said to Dominic, "I should go. I have to work."

Dominic said, "I'll drop you off."

Chiara replied, "I'd like that."

After they grabbed a quick breakfast, Dominic said, "I need a shower. Care to join me?"

Chiara said, "I'd love to."

He led her into the bathroom. While in the shower, he kissed her as he washed her. Under the warm water, they were intimate. As they got out, Chiara said, "I should go."

Dominic asked her, "What time do you get off work?"

She replied, "At four."

Then they got dressed and left. As they pulled up in front of the boutique where she worked, he said, "I'll pick you up at four."

She said, "I'd like that." They shared a long, passionate kiss; then she got out.

Chapter Thirty

As fate would have it, while in her hometown to visit her ailing grandmother, Angie had an encounter with a handsome young man from her past: Duvan Estrada. A long time ago, Duvan and Angie had dated seriously. Just as Duvan had hoped to propose to Angie, she had abruptly ended their relationship to be with another man, Dominic Cardenas. Duvan had been extremely disappointed. He had secretly felt that he was the right man for Angie.

Chapter Thirty-One

It was a hot night in Arielle, and the place to be was the trendy new nightclub. Cisco Cardenas sat at a corner booth. Across from him was his good friend, Caio Domingos. It was just after eight, and the bar was hopping.

Paloma and Patricia Kayano came in. Paloma looked around and said to Patricia, "This is where we need to be."

Patricia replied, "Hmm, hmm."

They found a corner table. Caio had been watching them and said to Cisco, "I'll be back."

Cisco said, "Alright."

He watched as Caio slowly made his way over to where Paloma and Patricia were sitting. He smiled to himself and thought about Janna.

He slipped into the back, took out his cell phone, and called Janna. When she answered, he said, "Hey, baby girl. I was just thinking about you."

Janna smiled to herself and said, "I was thinking about you too."

After a brief silence, Cisco asked Janna, "What are you up to tonight?"

Janna replied, "Oh, not much. Just relaxing."

Cisco said, "I'm coming over right now."

Janna said, "Yay! I'll see you soon."

Chapter Thirty-Two

Dominic was having a great time with Chiara. The more he got to know her, the more he liked her and the more attracted to her he became. For her part, Chiara was enjoying being with Dominic. He was quite unlike the other men she had dated. He was very affectionate and protective, and she felt safe with him. She was well aware that he was married, but she got the feeling he wasn't happy.

Chapter Thirty-Three

It was just after eight on Monday night when Angie returned home. After the long drive, she was quite tired. As soon as she got into the apartment, she called out to Dominic—once, twice, three times—with no answer. She went over to the answering machine that was beeping and played the messages. There was one from her good friend, Jacey Arias, asking her to call right away.

Afterward, Angie went into the bedroom, but Dominic was nowhere to be found. After a quick shower, she called Jacey.

Jacey said, "Well, it's about time I reached you."

Angie replied, "Yeah, I was away taking care of my grandmother. I just got back."

Jacey asked, "Oh, how is your grandmother?"

Angie sat at the kitchen counter and said, "Well, she's better now. My brother is with her."

Jacey said, "I'm glad she's feeling better."

Angie asked, "So what's been going on?"

Jacey thought for a minute and then said, "Well, I think we should talk in private. How about tomorrow morning at the diner?"

Angie said, "Sure, that sounds good."

Angie suddenly wondered if something was wrong with Jacey as she hung up.

Chapter Thirty-Four

The latest hot gossip around Arielle was about a certain couple. In Arielle, when one wanted to hear the latest juicy gossip, one just had to go to the beauty salon or the barber shop.

On this day, Cisco Cardenas sat in the barbershop. The barber said to him quietly, "I saw your father last night, and he wasn't alone."

Cisco looked at him and asked, "What do you mean?"

The barber glanced around quickly and said, "I saw your father with a young lady, looking quite cozy."

Cisco shook his head and said, "No, I don't believe that. It must have been someone else."

The barber said, "Oh, I'm sure it was him."

Cisco refused to believe that his father was running around with some girl. In the back of his mind, he knew that if what he was just told was true, it would definitely not be the first time. He knew then and there that there was only one way to find out the truth.

Chapter Thirty-Five

Cisco and his father sat in his home study. There was an uneasy silence between the two of them. As Cisco looked over at his father, he thought about what his barber had told him the day before. At first, he didn't want to believe it, but then Cisco thought back to when he was a young boy and what he had seen. He decided to get the truth from his father.

He took a deep breath and said to Dominic, "My barber told me yesterday that he saw you the other day with a young lady."

Dominic sat up straight in his chair and said, "He had no right to tell you that."

Cisco was not about to play games with his father. He said to him, "Dad, just tell me the truth."

Dominic stood up and walked over to the fireplace. As he turned to face Cisco, he asked, "Just what do you want to know?"

Cisco leaned back in his chair and said, "I want to know who this girl is and how long it's been going on."

Dominic said, "She's no one you know; the rest is my business."

This annoyed Cisco. He stood up and said to Dominic, "You just lost me." With that, he stormed out.

Dominic sat at his desk. All he wanted was to see Chiara.

Chapter Thirty-Six

Cisco was having a hard time dealing with what his father had told him. He had thought his father was the greatest guy for so long, but now he wasn't so sure. He was quite disappointed that his father had not been honest with him. He thought about his mother, Angie. He suddenly wondered if she knew. He felt a sudden need to tell her. She deserved to know.

Later that day, he called her. When she picked up, he said, "Hey, Mom."

She replied, "Hi, sweetie. What's going on?"

Cisco said, "I really need to speak to you."

She said, "Alright." By his tone, she could tell that it was something serious.

An hour later, she was buzzing him in as they sat at the dining table.

Chapter Thirty-Seven

After Cisco left his mother, all he wanted was to see Janna. Sitting in his car, he pulled out his phone and called her. When she answered, he said, "Hey, baby."

She replied, "Hi, honey."

He said, "I really need to see you right now."

She responded, "Sure. Come on over."

When Cisco saw Janna, he decided that nothing else in the world mattered. He stepped into her apartment and pulled her into his arms. He lowered his mouth to hers and kissed her passionately. She wrapped her arms around him and returned his kisses.

Chapter Thirty-Eight

It was at this time that a handsome stranger from Angie's past was about to arrive. It was a week after her talk with Cisco. Angie was sitting at the kitchen table when the phone rang. It was Duvan Estrada.

The story was that in college, Duvan and Angie had dated seriously. Duvan had expected that after college, they would get engaged. However, a month before they graduated, Angie met another man, Dominic Cardenas. She smiled to herself now and said, "Hello, Duvan."

She was surprised and pleased to hear from him. While Angie was looking after her grandmother, she had run into Duvan. Over coffee in the local bakery, they had caught up with each other. Even after all these years, there was still a lot of chemistry between them.

Chapter Thirty-Nine

Duvan Estrada was the powerful President and CEO of Estrada Enterprises. At twenty-one, he graduated from a well-known college at the top of his class. He continued on to get his MBA. His father was Fernando Estrada, the owner of Estrada Hotels and Resorts.

Duvan was 6'2" and extremely handsome. He had a deep tan, coal-black eyes, and jet-black hair. He was the oldest of three, with two younger sisters, Luciana and Valeria, who were both dancers.

Chapter Forty

On Friday night, after a steamy date with Chiara, Dominic Cardenas sat in his living room. As he sat there staring out the glass window, Dominic came to realize two very important facts: one was that he was in love with Chiara, and the other was that his marriage was over. He knew exactly what his next move should be. He now wrestled in his mind with how to tell Angie and his children.

Chapter Forty-One

Cisco and Janna were having a great time. They had just finished a lovely dinner at a romantic new restaurant. Now they were back in his new apartment. Day by day, things were progressing very naturally between Cisco and Janna. Cisco found himself falling deeper and deeper in love with Janna every time they were together. Janna felt she had finally found the man of her dreams in Cisco.

On this night, while they were lying together on the couch, Cisco said to Janna in a sexy, low voice, "Janna, baby, I love you." Janna turned in his arms to face him, and, touching his face tenderly, she said, "I love you too, Cisco." And they kissed. It was a kiss full of promised passion and commitment.

Chapter Forty-Two

Dominic and Angie sat at the kitchen table. There was an uneasy silence between them. Dominic took a deep breath and then said to Angie, "I want out of our marriage. I want a divorce." Although Angie had had her suspicions all along and had prepared herself, it still stung.

After a long silence, Dominic said, "First thing tomorrow morning, I will start looking at apartments." Angie said quietly, "Yes, I think that would be best."

Later that day, Cisco came over. As soon as he saw his mother, he could tell something was bothering her. As they sat at the kitchen table, he asked her, "Mom, what's wrong?" Angie said, "Your father and I are getting a divorce." Cisco sat up straight in his chair and asked, "What?!" Angie said, "Yeah, you heard right." Cisco leaned back in his chair. It was hard for him to grasp the fact that after all these years of marriage, his parents were divorcing. He stood up and went into the backyard. Angie watched him walk back and forth. It was what he always did when he needed space to think. After a few minutes, he came back in and sat down. He said to Angie, "I will be here for you." Angie smiled and reached over to touch his face. An hour later, he left.

Chapter Forty-Three

Two days later, Duvan called Angie. She was coping with the fact that her marriage was over. At this time, she took small comfort in the fact that she had Duvan. Over dinner that night, Angie told Duvan. Afterward, he said, "Well, it's his loss." He reached over and took her hand. As Angie looked at Duvan, she saw the love that she had seen all those years before. At that moment, she decided that all she wanted now was to be with Duvan. For his part, Duvan felt a strong desire to care for and protect Angie.

Chapter Forty-Four

It was a warm night in Arielle, and the happening place to be was the Estrada mansion. It was a huge party to mark the end of summer. As the guests arrived, they were directed straight to the backyard. There was a setup playing some lively tunes. There was an Olympic-sized pool and a tennis court. Servers walked around with platters of hors d'oeuvres.

Among the guests, there was a mystery man. He sat in the far corner, just taking in the festivities. People were dancing and mingling. Everyone was well aware of the fact that once fall came, it meant that the holidays were not far away.

Chapter Forty-Five

Just after eleven, the guests started to make their way out slowly. Everyone had a great time. The night was turning misty, and the full moon was drifting in and out of the clouds. A light rain made the remaining guests head into the mansion.

Duvan and Angie had slipped away to the guest house set back on the property. All evening, Duvan had wanted to be alone with Angie. Once they were settled in the guest house, Duvan wasted no time in showing Angie his true intentions. He took her by the hand and led her into his bedroom. It was an extremely passionate night. Duvan showed Angie a few times that not only did he know what to do in bed, but he did it quite well—four times.

Afterward, they lay in each other's arms, quite satisfied. It wasn't long before they fell asleep in each other's arms.

Chapter Forty-Six

The mystery man slipped away, quite sure that he hadn't been seen. His only purpose for attending the evening's festivities was to observe the people he would soon be living with quietly. Once he was satisfied, he left. He had some business to take care of before he made his move to Arielle.

Chapter Forty-Seven

A few days later, Kaue Araujo called Patricio Kayano. Patricio said, "Hey, Kaue. What's up?" As Kaue sat at his kitchen counter, he asked Patricio, "Did you happen to see that strange guy?" Patricio said, "No, I don't believe I did."

Both men couldn't figure out who the mystery man was or where he had come from. It was only a matter of time before they would be introduced to the mystery man.

Chapter Forty-Eight

It was at this time that Cisco sat down with his father, Dominic. The two men had a real heart-to-heart talk. Afterward, they decided they would work together to repair their relationship.

Chapter Forty-Nine

It was a very romantic night for Duvan and Angie after all these years of being apart. While they were lying together on the couch in Duvan's living room, Duvan said in his sexy, low voice, "Angie, baby, I love you." Those were the words Angie had waited so long to hear. She turned in his arms and touched his face, saying, "I love you, too, Duvan."

He kissed her lightly at first, then their kisses deepened. Soon after, he stood up and pulled her up. He led her into his bedroom, and the night got ten times hotter. There was a lot of tenderness and intimacy between them. It was only in the wee hours of the morning when they fell asleep in each other's arms.

Chapter Fifty

It was a warm night in Arielle, and romance hung in the air. It was the night that Cisco Cardenas and Janna Harlow would always remember. After months of careful planning, Cisco Cardenas proposed to Janna Harlow in the most romantic way. When she said "yes," he slipped the huge diamond ring onto her finger, which fit perfectly. There were a lot of cheers and congratulations for the happy couple.

He stood at a distance, not wanting to be seen. He observed the festivities. Everyone was so happy, but their happiness wouldn't last long. Just that thought brought a smile to his face.